WITHDRAWN

Carroll Community College
1601 Washington Road
Westminster, M 21157

Delirium

D0833471

Delirium

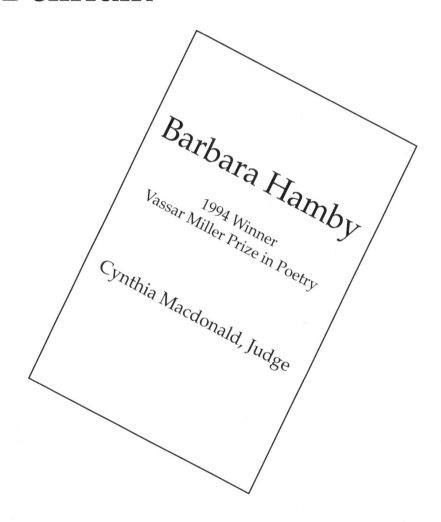

Barbara Hamby

1994 Winner
Vassar Miller Prize in Poetry

Cynthia Macdonald, Judge

University of North Texas Press
Denton, Texas

© 1995 Barbara Hamby

All rights reserved.
Printed in the United States of America

First Edition 1995

10 9 8 7 6 5 4 3 2 1

Permissions

University of North Texas Press
Post Office Box 13856
Denton, Texas 76203

The paper used in this book meets the minimum requirements of the
American National Standard for Permanence of Paper for
Printed Library materials, z39.48.1984.
Binding materials have been chosen for durability.

Library of Congress Cataloging-in-Publication Data

Hamby, Barbara, 1952–
Delirium : poems / by Barbara Hamby.
        p.   cm.
ISBN 1-57441-002-4 (cloth : alk. paper). — ISBN 1-57441-003-2
(paper : alk. paper)
I. Title.
PS3558.A4216D45   1995b   95-33311
811'.54—dc20   CIP

Grateful acknowledgment is made to the following publications in which some of these poems have appeared:

Another Chicago Magazine: "The Language of Bees" and "My Sin."

Confrontation: "Killer Bees Are Sighted in Belize" and "Regarding Insects in General."

The Iowa Review: "James Atkins, Irlandese," "The Ovary Tattoo," "St. Anthony of the Floating Larynx," and "Toska."

The Ledge: "Ova" and "Betrothal in B minor."

Mississippi Mud: "The Beatification of St. Lucy."

Negative Capability: "To Italy," "Keats' Disease Addresses Him in the Voice of Mr. Lovelace, Nemesis of Clarissa Harlowe in the Eponymous Novel Which Keats Finishes Reading (in Nine Volumes) the Night Before He Leaves Naples," "Dr. Clark Examines Keats upon His Arrival in Rome," "Signora Angeletti Discusses Her Two Boarders (with recipe)," "Lt. Isaac Marmaduke Elton and Keats on La Principessa Borghese (née Pauline Bonaparte), Marble and Flesh," "The Autopsy of John Keats," and "Dust."

New Laurel Review: "The Dada of Bees."

The Paris Review: "Delirium" and "Nose."

Southern Humanities Review: "Eating Bees."

Western Humanities Review: "Deception" and "St. Clare's Underwear."

Some of the poems in this volume appeared in two chapbooks *Eating Bees* (Pittsburgh: New Sins Press, 1992) and *Skin* (Eugene, Oregon: Silverfish Review Press, 1995), which was winner of the Gerald Cable Poetry Chapbook Award.

"The Language of Bees," "The Ovary Tattoo," and "St. Anthony of the Floating Larynx" appeared in the anthology *Isle of Flowers* (Anhinga Press, 1995).

The writing of these poems was made possible by a grant from the Florida Arts Council and the Florida Department of State, Division of Cultural Affairs.

for David,
innamorato mio

Contents

I

II

III

The Autopsy of John Keats

I

The Language of Bees

The language of bees contains 76 distinct words for stinging,
     distinguishes between a prick, puncture, and mortal wound,
elaborates on cause and effect as in a sting made to retaliate,
     irritate, insinuate, infuriate, incite, rebuke, annoy,
     nudge, anger, poison, harangue.
The language of bees has 39 words for queen—regina apiana,
     empress of the hive, czarina of nectar, maharani of the ovum,
     sultana of stupor, principessa of dark desire.
The language of bees includes 22 words for sunshine,
Two for rain—big water and small water, so that a man urinating
     on an azalea bush in the full fuchsia of April
     has the linguistic effect of a light shower in September.
For man, two words—roughly translated—"hands" and "feet,"
     the first with the imperialistic connotation of beekeeper,
     the second with the delicious resonance of bareness.
All colors are variations on yellow, from the exquisite
     sixteen-syllable word meaning "diaphanous golden fall,"
     to the dirty ochre of the bitter pollen
     stored in the honeycomb and used by bees for food.

The language of bees is a language of war. For what is peace
     without strife but the boredom of enervating day-after-day,
     obese with sweetness, truculent with ennui?
Attack is delightful to bees, who have hundreds of verbs
     embracing strategy, aim, location, velocity:
     swift, downward swoop to stun an antagonist,
     brazen, kamikaze strike for no gain but momentum.
Yet stealth is essential to bees, for they live to consternate
     their enemies, flying up pant legs, hovering in grass.
No insect is more secretive than the bee, for they have two
     thousand words describing the penetralia of the hive:
     octagonal golden chamber of unbearable moistness,

opaque tabernacle of nectar,
sugarplum of polygonal waxy walls.

The language of bees is a language of aeronautics,
        for they have wings—transparent, insubstantial,
        black-veined like the fall of an exotic iris.
For they are tiny dirigibles, aviators of orchard and field.
For they have ambition, cunning, and are able to take direct aim.
For they know how to leave the ground, to drift, hover, swarm,
        sail over the tops of trees.
The language of bees is a musical dialect, a full, humming
        congregation of hallelujahs and amens,
        at night blue and disconsolate,
        in the morning bright and bedewed.
The language of bees contains lavish adjectives
        praising the lilting fertility of their queen:
        fat, red-bottomed progenitor of millions,
        luscious organizer of coitus,
        gelatinous distributor of love.
The language of bees is in the jumble of leaves before rain,
        in the quiet night rustle of small animals,
        for it is eloquent and vulgar in the same mouth,
        and though its wound is sweet it can be distressing,
        as if words could not hurt or be meant to sting.

Betrothal in B minor

All women bewail the betrothal of any woman,
beamy-eyed, bedazzled, throwing a fourth finger

about like a marionette. Worse than marriage
in many ways, an engagement, be it moments or millennia,

is a morbid exercise in hope, a mirage, a romance
befuddled by magazine photographs of lips, eyebrows,

brassieres, B-cups, bromides, bimbos bedaubed
with kohl, rouged, bespangled, beaded, beheaded,

really, because a woman loses the brain
she was born with if she believes for a moment

she of all women will escape enslavement of mind,
milk, mooring, the machinations of centuries,

to arrive in a blissful, benign, borderless
Brook Farm where men are uxorious, mooning,

bewitched, besotted, bereft of all beastly,
beer-guzzling qualities. Oh, no, my dear

mademoiselle, marriage is no *déjeuner sur l'herbe*,
no bebop with Little Richard for eternity,

no bedazzled buying spree at Bergdorf or Bendel,
no clinch on the beach with Burt Lancaster.

Although it is sometimes all these things, it is
more often, to quote la Marquise de Merteuil, "War,"

but war against the beastliness within that makes
us want to behave, eat beets, buy beef at the market,

wash with Fab, betray our beautiful minds
tending to the personal hygiene of midgets.

My God, Beelzebub himself could not have manufactured
a more Machiavellian maneuver to bedevil an entire

species than this benighted impulse to replicate
ourselves ad nauseam in the confines of a prison

so perfect, bars are redundant. Even in the Bible
all that begetting and begatting only led to misery,

morbidity, Moses, and murder. I beseech you,
my sisters, let's cease, desist, refrain,

take a breather, but no one can because we are
driven by tiny electrical sparks that bewilder,

befog, beguile, becloud our angelic intellect.
Besieged by hormones, we are stalked by a disease

unnamed, a romantic glaucoma. We are doomed to die,
bespattered and besmirched beneath the dirt,

under the pinks and pansies of domestic domination.
Oh, how I loathe you—perfect curtains, exquisite chairs,

crème brûlée of my dreams. Great gods of pyromania,
begrudge not your handmaiden, your fool, the flames

that fall from your fiery sky, for my dress is tattered
and my shoes are different colors, blue and red.

Ova

Oval, hard-shelled or soft, eaten for breakfast,
bought in dozens, six to a row, two rows, brown or white,

subject of riddles (which came first), subject of fables,
to wit the goose and the golden one, symbol of Christ

in Piero della Francesca's sublime painting in which he
suspends an ostrich's over the impassive sphere

of the Virgin's head, not that the attendant angels
with their buttery curls or saints notice, so busy are they

studying the tiles and the shine on Federigo da Montfeltro's
armor and bald head. A chicken lays one at a time,

a fish hundreds, a queen bee mates with a dozen or so drones
and commences to lay them for over a year. And think

of the discrete parts: the shells—is there a more perfect shape
in nature? Certainly not, according to Carl Gustavovich Fabergé,

whose begemmed and enameled concoctions delighted
the hemophilia-carrying scions of the frayed remnants

of imperial Russia; or the white, pellucid, slippery albumen
that, whipped to hysterical heights, becomes meringue,

snowy chapeaux of fruity tarts and pies; and the yolk—
round, golden orb that mixed with water and hue and affixed

to board can become *La Primavera* or *The Birth of Venus*.
Scramble it, bake it, pickle it, fry it—over easy,

sunny-side up. Caviar and champagne, omelet, quiche, frittata.
Everyone emanates from one, little zygotes, piling on one

confusing cell after another but forever beset by an atavistic
longing to be once more oval with a heart of gold.

Eating Bees

Empty churches drone
      with the low buzzing
of angry bees, angels
      bickering with lost souls,
fishwives in the holy
      market of noise.
No silence is sacred
      to these downy criminals
seeking revenge
      on bare feet in summer,
we go to the beach,
      dive in, and it's all bees;
their wings tickle
      our faces like water,
and when our ears are full,
      they spill out, breakers
of transparent blue rushing upon us,
      wave upon wave,
surge upon swell,
      until our skulls are filled,
like shells, with sound.

The Ovary Tattoo

Etched on my abdomen like a botanical illustration
is the reproductive paraphernalia of a flower

or *facsimile animalis*, the oviduct named for
Gabriello Fallopio, Italian anatomist,

no artist but a careful researcher, his vellum
untouched by the meandering entrails on the table,

untidy detritus of tissue and blood, a reminder that,
above all, God is Albrecht Dürer, an expert draftsman,

peculiar in his tastes, untidy but organized, peripatetic,
not particularly ecstatic in the connubial state and bent

on a sort of subtle revenge, for bare form tells all,
the apparatus itself like antlers or the antennae

of some marvelous insect, a bee, *apis mirabilis*,
yet on its side becomes a spilled cup or pincers

and darker still when capsized, an anchor,
ponderous iron, pulling hull, mast, sail, sailors

into the unfathomable bowels of primal craving. Some say
love is a cave, unlit and mysterious, or do they say

it's a long corridor in a lavish French château
lined with mirrors, icy laughter caught on the dripping

crystals of chandeliers? I forget. Perhaps it's both,
a declivity and *une galerie des glaces*, goldleaf nymphs

bearing platters of light into musty caverns beneath
the castle, the sheen of their skin in candlelight

belying the bastinado of blood, evil and completely
seductive, Scheherazade on a cellular level, because

if there is one thing about love that I will never
understand, it's how pale it is, unaccustomed to daylight,

yet how it seems to live in the mad drumming of the blood
and then can sit in the chest like a high-toned cleric who, upon

closing his lesson book, crawls along the intestinal tract
like a transvestite demagogue, preaching to the E. coli

and the mutating cells, "Replicate, breed, multiply, procreate,
propagate, proliferate, make more babies for God,"

until every square inch of ground is awash in humanity,
the mad pulse of a trillion aortas, the tick, throb,

stroke, thump, pant of blood rising like a deep jungle moan:
we are hungry, we are angry, we are helpless, we are here.

Venus Speaks

—for Patricia Rose

One person's Venus is not another's, and "Thank God,"
as my mother used to say in vastly different circumstances,

"Because the world would be a dull place indeed
if we were all the same," so it's a good thing

that Botticelli, Rubens and Pablo Pizzicato
were not working from a photograph, ludicrous idea,

seeing as how Venus is a metaphor and a classical one at that,
but an idea that has absorbed artists for several thousand years

and more if you count primitive fertility goddesses,
adorable lumps of sticky dirt, pronounced pudenda

relaying the point of the aesthetic act, though perhaps
I am wrong about her being anything more than an excuse to paint

the unclothed female form, really an exquisite concoction
no matter what the prevailing mode, and whether one prefers

the Vampire Aphrodites of Paris or like Gaugin opts
for a more relaxed goddess, they are female one and all, women,

and by definition lovely, because even an irritable woman
has her charms or how could Lucas Cranach have made a career

of painting his slender, discrete, malicious deities?
His is not a classical Venus, marble-hipped, impassive,

or an Italian goddess, bovine-eyed, dreamy-skinned,
or Rubenesque, a rippling giantess. No, her digits

are too spidery, her earlobes overlanguorous, eyes
almost Oriental, slanted with demonic knowledge,

and her little Wiener Schnitzel, Cupid, who Cranach often posed
at Venus's feet with a honeycomb in his hands, vengeful bees

circling his curly pate, he is more naughty lumpkin
than demigod and in agony because of apiary misdemeanors.

Our beauty does not give a philosophical fig. She smirks
at us, wine-velvet chapeau tilted, sly mouth arched

in what could be called—by the manifestly unobservant or dull—
a smile, but you and I are too sophisticated for that.

My God, we've been to Berlin, can say Constantinople, have eaten
things our nine-year-old selves would have committed hara-kiri

upon simply touching, we know about Wittgenstein and his brother
and lots else besides, so Cranach's Venus speaks to us

in a way that Titian's never could, nor Manet's with her
little black cat; this is a woman with whom we could be friends

but not too close, because Cupid and those bees
are the subtext of something, and Venus is clutching

the branch of a tree heavy with perfect fruit, as if to say,
"You're hungry? Have an apple," and we've heard that one before.

Invention

I am personally indebted to antiquity because if it were left
to me nothing would have been invented. We would still be chasing

boars and clubbing them to death. No, that's too refined.
We'd still be eating grass and grubbing for worms.

How did they think up all that stuff? I'm not talking
about painting or literature or music. That's easy.

What could be more natural than sitting around a campfire
telling stories and then rhyming to make them easier to remember

or having two or three people take different parts?
Voilà, poetry and theatre. I'm talking about bread.

Who thought of grinding wheat and mixing it with mold?
Forget bread. I can't get past wheat. Wheat must have been a weed

once. Who walked up to wheat and thought about growing
a whole field of it, picking it, smashing it together,

adding water, throwing it on a fire? Who were these
proto-chemists, these Neanderthal Marie and Pierre Curies

who harnessed the grain? The leap from throwing rocks at birds
and grilling them on a spit to Safeway is too great for me,

which leads to another subject if one picks up reading material
in supermarkets. Recently I discovered that alien civilizations

do not vacation on Earth anymore because we are too bellicose
and vulgar. Well, whose fault is it anyway? Anyone who thinks

that buffoons such as we could have thought up wheat,
not to mention architecture, axles, armor, artillery

is not taking his Lithium. There would still be about 250 of us
in caves somewhere in France if someone with big silver eyes

hadn't been buzzing around the universe, bored, sentimental,
and decided to stop and help us along. Next thing you know

there's agriculture, horticulture, apiculture. It's the only
logical explanation and if it weren't for the CIA,

everyone would agree with me. However, scientists in Russia,
Argentina, and the north of England (top-notch men,

every one of them) theorize that not only did the Andromedans
show us a few tricks, they also mated with the indigenous

species. Yuck, you might say, if they think we're creepy now,
just imagine what our manners were like ten or twenty thousand

years ago, though come to think of it, I doubt the alien *haute
bourgeoisie* was patrolling the outer reaches of the universe.

According to a test devised by these scientists, you can tell
if you are descended from extraterrestrials by certain physical

characteristics, such as blond hair, slender fingers,
musical ability (especially singing), big eyes, blue eyes,

which all point to a racially pure colony in Sweden
or Schleswig-Holstein for a few thousand years

and are somewhat reminiscent of our recent troubles in Europe
and Japan. I, for one, would like to toast an inventor:

Tchin, tchin, Dom Perignon, who said when he discovered champagne, "My God, I am drinking the stars."

Regarding Insects in General

Small, some are tiny,
    like the silver, almost transparent gnat,
flying up noses and in general a nuisance,
    especially in numbers,
or malevolent disease-carrying scourges—
    ticks, mosquitoes, fleas,
nearly halving the population of Europe,
    traveling incognito in ships
    from London to Lisbon to Rome.
Yet the order Lepidoptera flutters by
    on diaphanous wings,
phosphorescent blue and black,
    and moths the size of hummingbirds
feed on white ginger in the warm September twilight
    or beetles, muse to the Egyptians
    and John, Paul, George and Ringo.
They descend on the world,
    devouring fields of wheat and barley,
closets of cashmere sweaters, fruit on trees,
    food in cupboards. We become them—
Peter Lorre in *M*, the Fly,
    or waking one morning in Prague,
feeling more than slightly hung over, wondering,
    "What have I done to make me feel like this?"

Killer Bees Are Sighted in Belize

My sister is uncovering a post-Classical Mayan hut
        in a Belize jungle when she looks overhead
        and sees a black cloud in the distance.
"Rain," says the bush doctor, who is also working
        on the dig.
"Rain," says the fat archeologist from Yale,
        who is emperor of the dig.
"Rain," say Catherine, Colin, and Jill,
        the three children who live next to the dig
        and play at the site every day.
"Rain?" asks the Peace Corps worker,
        who is growing a nest of hair on her chin
        and is so weird that even village people,
        who have nothing, make fun of her.
But it is not rain. Thor is completely uninvolved
        in this phenomenon.
"Not rain," says the bush doctor,
        scratching his genitals,
and the day goes on with everyone wishing for rain
        to mitigate the candent tropical sun,
but wishing for so much more, really, that it is lost
        in the low rumbling of desire
that reverberates through the collective
        unconsciousness huddled around that particular acre
        in the universe.
The rotund king of the site wants a gin and tonic
        more intensely than he has ever wanted anything,
but after that he desires deification
        as the Great God of American Archeology,
with, of course, all the attendant praise,
        jealousy, backbiting, subterfuge, and power.
His wife, a pretty if not too intelligent woman,
        wants a hot bath with lavender salts

and a husband who is not a megalomaniac
	or who, at the very least, is not seventy pounds overweight.
The bush doctor wants to have sex with the queen
	consort, with my sister, with DeeDee
	the cheerleader from Indiana,
with any woman within a five mile radius
	except the Peace Corps worker,
and has for the past month been disemboweling chickens
	for haruspical purposes
	that have not been altogether successful.
Catherine, Colin, and Jill dream of living in Florida,
	in Disney World, to be precise.
The Peace Corps worker, aware of her inability
	to be even remotely like the others
	and long past worrying about it,
would like to lie down on the jungle floor
	and fall into a sleep, deep and utterly dark,
	beyond thought, beyond reason, beyond inclination
and falling, finally land in a remote if familiar room
	where reside not only her present group but
the Big Buffalo, the Kahuna of Unconsciousness,
	with his nattering, babbling, googol of minions,
who are quarreling, squabbling, stabbing,
	achieving a level of mayhem unrivaled
	in our relatively repressed plane of endeavor.
Pushing her way through the anarchic pandemonium,
	she stands beard-to-beard
with the big guy himself—brillo head, Brobdingnagian
	abdomen—bulging eyeballs
	less than an inch from hers and pleads,
"Help me," to which he replies,
	"Look up, there's danger everywhere."

Toska

I still haven't forgiven Natasha for marrying Pierre,
not actually for marrying him but for being happy with him.

How could she, after Prince Andrei? I know, I know,
life must go on, but I want something finer for her,

beyond wiping snotty noses and hanging on his every word.
Not a modern epilogue with everyone dead or bitterly unhappy

or both, but something else, a sense of longing or ache
for which there is no word in English. In Russian

there is the word *toska*, which describes an undefined desire,
a sense that what you need and want most is elsewhere

or doesn't exist at all. English wouldn't have a word
for such a feeling, for ours is a language of materialism first,

a language in which ideally everything you need is obtainable because
everything is tangible. French is another language which

would probably not have a word like *toska* though there is the
conditionnel antérieur, or the tense of regret, yet regret

is not what I want Natasha to feel nor melancholy. The French word
ennui is better than our *boredom* but still not quite right.

At the Tower of Babel when God first gave us languages,
what was it like? Everyone jabbering like crazy, trying to find

someone who understood what he was saying and then sorting
themselves out? Or was it like being struck by lightning—

nothing the same, bricklayers contemplating their mortar
and not knowing what it was for, much less what it was called?

This seems more likely. I can see people wandering off—
befuddled husbands knowing their wives but not knowing them

at the same time, and friends passing each other and remembering
that they are friends but not knowing what a friend is.

How wonderful it had been for a time, planning the tower,
deciding on its diameter and circumference, the philosophy

of it all. There had even been a delegation whose entire function
was composing a speech to be delivered when they finally

came face to face with God. Alas, these poor pundits
later migrated to a land just north of the Alps and developed

a maddening portmanteau language that when faced with a miracle
such as the Assumption of the Virgin into heaven on a cloud

of angels came up with *Himmelfahrt Maria*, which, though not
precisely untrue, reveals no sense of God as a patriarchal vacuum

or the shock of the Apostles below and their desolation at losing her.
Desolation is a good word, but not what I want for Natasha,

nor is it *toska*, because what she most needed existed once
but is gone as is that inclination to converse with God.

Arpeggio, Archipelago, Arpège

Listening to "A Variation on a Theme by Paganini"
  by Paderewski, played by Rubinstein,
  my husband and I dine elegantly

On a concoction of his own creation,
  a cassoulet of the sort eaten by Basques
  but transformed by the French into something sublime.

This is a time when we wish people would drop by
  to see us with our Bordeaux, our candlelight, our damask.
  This is the real we, in love, drinking wine

Listening to Paganini via Paderewski via Rubinstein
  who, collectively, are becoming pyrotechnical,
  burning the keyboard, the piano, invented in 1742 by

Giacomo Pianissimo but in reality sixty years later by
  Ludwig von Liechtenstein. "Is that an arpeggio?"
  my darling asks. Drawing on my quickly receding

Musical education, I flounder in the Rio Bordeaux
  and he says, "Arpeggio, archipelago, Arpège," three words,
  I realize, by which my whole childhood could be summed up—

Hours of painful, pointless endeavor on the piano, plunking,
  plinking, plonking my way through Debussy, Beethoven (aka
  Liechtenstein) and the ever divine Wolf-Wolf,

My fate sealed by an abysmal lack of hand-eye coordination,
  combined with the concentration span of a tennis ball,
  in a living room in Honolulu, capital city of arguably

The Queen of Archipelagos, strung out in the Pacific
  like a necklace of palm trees, plumeria, pikake, shell
  ginger, birds, the aforementioned room ruled by

My mother, Madame Arpège, her scent permeating my memories,
  fast flaking from the walls like a particularly unsuccessful
  experiment by Leonardo, well, not him but perhaps his

Demented second cousin. Where was I? Oh, yes, here, again
  in my lovely present, with my husband, a man of penetration,
  of great physical beauty, a poetic man, pink in places,

Who, I am convinced, was created just for me in the factory
  of Romantic Reverberations, which I find myself quivering
  with at the moment, the bees of lust swarming up my spine,

Is it wine or music or the mayhem of the moment
  that has contrived to befuddle my mental workings, my lips
  drawn to his, the fireflies of desire flimmering in my throat,

Eyes opaque with something I am reaching to define, my mind
  like a wasp, maddened, trapped in the hot car of my brain—
  "Scales," I cry, and fall again into that disorder of arms.

I Hear a Samba

Who says the night is quiet is not listening,
      because it's three a.m. again and I'm looking out
at the same white, moonlit room,
      music whispering from the fillings in my teeth,
music with a beat: one, two, three,
      South American, salsa, sombrero, cha-cha-cha.
This is when all my mistakes visit me,
      rising like vermin from the door cracks,
closets, flue. "Dance with us," they scream,
      the yoga teacher, the artist, the pianist,
the antivivisectionist. Their dance is witless,
      they sway their hips in zombie abandon,
eyes glassy, mouths slightly open,
      fingers snapping, heels slamming on the floorboards.
I look over at my husband, face like an angel,
      how can he sleep with all this racket?
"La cucaracha," they yell, "olé."
      I beg them to go away. "We can't," they sing,
one-two-three. "Shut up," I scream. "I hate you."
      "You liked us once," they sneer, prancing like the reindeer
in my third-grade Christmas play. My darling stirs.
      I couldn't have liked them. Who are they?
Who was I when I knew them?
      What mental disease gripped my psyche?
"Come back to us," they call.
      "You're married," I say. "You have children."
"We're married," they cry. "We have children."
      They take it up like an anthem:
"We're married. We have children. We're married.
      We have children." They spin faster and faster,
their faces red, then purple, then black
      as the honeyed night,
pulling me down into the sweet sheets of sleep.

My Sin

All sex is said to emanate from scent.
Between the cover of sweat and
Chanel Number 19, it is there like a
Devious giant, attractive, derisive,
Elemental. Disguise it with perfume,
Flower it into submission, mask its
Genital allure, but there's no
Hiding this signor—amorous,
Insistent, turning ambition into
Jello, ambivalence into a secret, sick
Kind of longing you can't help, but
Loathe, yet there he is big, wide
Monkey smile on his silly face,
Natty mustachioes, a rouge spot
On each cheek. To run away to
Paris with him is all you want.
"Qui est la femme cuckoo?" I
Reply, "C'est moi." Why not?
St. Peter's going to blanch at
The sight of me anyhow, really of
Us. I can hear him now, "Vanity,
Vanity, all is blah, blah, blah."
Well, there's no substitute for
Ecstasy, though many pretend as
You and I continue our bumbling if
Zealous court of *le petit mort*.

The Dada of Bees

Who, given the choice of being witty or good,
would not chose to be Oscar Wilde?
To make mistakes, yes, but to be quick
and to know what beauty is.
"Beauty and speed"—quite a credo,
more like Cocteau's heroine
on amphetamines than anything on which
to base your life,
and the divine Oscar ending up so badly
in prison for that silly prettyboy
and his great bully of a father.
Then after walking along the Seine,
beauty and health gone
but the muscle of irony intact.
And in the end what could be more
satisfying, for beauty abandons everyone,
and praise is like an inhalation,
sweet in the blood for a moment
and then forgotten in the flurry
of evil that buzzes around our heads.

A Farewell to Beekeeping

The French are so damned erotic. *Au revoir.*
      I ask you.
A woman has to stick out her chest as well as her chin
      to get in all the "r's,"
and what a sticky word like a piece of marzipan
      that looks like a peach or a bunch of grapes
but is really a little bit of sin, too sweet,
      not good for your teeth,
but everything you want, and of course you can't say,
      "Au revoir, bub,"
but must breathe à la Monroe, "Au revoir, mon chéri,"
      or "darling," or "mon petit poulet,"
      at the very least.
It's really love, love, love, or sex, sex, sex,
      depending on your point of view, or not,
if indeed Dr. Freud had any grip at all
      upon the perambulations of the psyche
      because both are the same, he says,
      which I don't believe for a minute.
My brain is quite tidy, thank you very much,
      although I do think about death all the time,
      usually when I'm having fun.
I'll say, "When I'm on my deathbed, will this be a moment
      I remember?"
That stupid bed, I've stretched the sheets on it
      a thousand times.
I never think of it when I'm depressed. Then it's show tunes.
      "My Boy Bill," or "Some Enchanted Evening."
I think of stupid Mitzi Gaynor with her stupid haircut
      and that ugly gingham ball gown.
Why waste a fabulous Italian basso on her, I ask God,
      and he replies,

"Because wearing the right dress does not matter.
        It's what's in your heart that counts."
I don't get this. For one thing it sounds too simple
        for God, and for another
Mitzi Gaynor's heart was the size of a walnut,
        if you ask me, and can't you have a great dress
        and a good heart?
Isn't the dress an indication of the state
        of your left and right ventricles?
Think of the Goose Girl. It doesn't have to be expensive.
        Could my mother have been so wrong?
        So hygiene isn't important?
These are some of the philosophical questions
        that consume me when I am not thinking
        about other things such as,
        "What's for dinner?" and "Liz Taylor married who?"
This morning I opened the paper and our plumber
        was on the front page, crazy, blood-smeared.
He had murdered his wife and her boyfriend.
        He was a great plumber, and funny,
        knew everything about roses.
Why is there this melancholy strain in the universe?
        It's so sad, and it won't go away.
Maybe it prepares us for our final exit,
        makes the bitter pill a little easier to choke down,
because every language has its own way of saying it:
        auf Wiedersehen, sayonara, goodbye.

II

James Atkins, Irlandese

Our apartment in Florence is like the set
      of a play by Molière.
Across the courtyard live the octogenarian
      Count and Countess degli Alessandri,
downstairs the sinister portiere
      and his beleaguered wife.
Is the count's brother plotting to kill him?
      It seems entirely plausible, given the archways
      and thick walls of our present hacienda.
"Somehow I doubt it," says my husband
      from behind *La Repubblica*,
      "seeing that they're both in their eighties."
We're in Italy. We have a courtyard with a fountain
      and lemon trees in pots, and a bedroom the size
      of Versailles with paintings in gold frames.
I lie in bed and gaze across the room at the portrait
      of a delicate young man or robust woman,
      the chiaroscuro being more *scuro* than *chiaro*,
And this cavalier (a he, I believe, rosy lips
      and languid eyes notwithstanding)
      wears a wide-brimmed hat with feathers
      and a lace jabot, glances seductively
      over his shoulder.
Attached to the gilt upper edge is a plaque,
      inscribed in rococo script:
      James Atkins, Irlandese.
Delirious, I say it over and over, "James Atkins,
      Irlandese. James Atkins, Irlandese."
Have I, like Stendhal in the great Franciscan
      church of Santa Croce, seen so much ravishing
      gloriousity that a wasting tuberculosis
      of the spirit has infected me?

After all, we are only three blocks from that very
          church, final resting place of Galileo,
          Michelangelo, and the frescoes of the life
          of St. Francis by Giotto, stellar pupil
          of Cenno dei Pepi, better known as Cimabue.
I myself have swooned in Santa Maria del Carmine
          before the fresco of the expulsion of Adam
          and Eve by Tommaso Guido, called Masaccio,
          which means Dirty Tom, though I don't know
          if this refers to a lack of hygiene or morals.
Fifteenth-century Florence was filled
          with these double-monikered artists:
          Sandro Filipepi, called Botticelli; Jacopo Carrucci,
          called Pontormo; and my favorite,
          Giovanni Antonio dei Bazzi, called Sodoma,
          for his predilection for young boys.
It's something you get used to, the young boys and
          everything having two names, for the English
          discovered Italy at the pinnacle of their empire.
Those crazy Inglese: why did they anglicize
          the perfectly pronounceable names of Italian cities?
Milano to Milan or Roma to Rome is understandable;
          when you have an empire to maintain,
          one syllable may be more efficient than two.
But Leghorn, I ask you? Why, when Livorno
          trips off the tongue like a mountain stream
          rippling over rocks?
And Firenze—a fierce word for this walled
          and contentious city—why change it to Florence?
And while we are in the interrogatory mood,
          I am reminded of another Anglo-Italian conundrum,
          posited by a fanciulla Veronese: "What's in a name?"
Well she should ask, for in her country we find not only
          the irlandesi, cinesi, and inglesi, but the indigenous
          milanesi and the livornesi and the fiorentini.
It becomes infinitely more complicated

when in Perugia we meet a perugino,
not simply the teacher of Raphael but a whole town
filled with perugini, and in Arezzo the aretini,
and in Montepulciano the poliziani.
But when we make our pilgrimage to Sansepolcro
to see Piero della Francesca's divine Resurrection,
we meet not the sansepolcresi but the biturgensi
and in Gubbio the eugubini, in Norcia the nursini.
And in Todi we find a city inhabited entirely
by tudertini, a word which brings to mind tubers
or truffles, tartufo in Italian, which sounds like Tartuffe,
character in a play by Molière, favorite of the Sun King,
born Jean-Baptiste Poquelin.

Le Stelle Sono Innumerevoli

You recognize this as a particularly Italian phrase,
  lyrical and mathematical at the same time,
for the numberlessness of the stars
  is like the invisibility of atoms,
not that your teacher speaks of anything
  but books and doors and windows.
The book is open, the book is shut,
  the door is open, the door is shut,
the window is open,
  and it is through this open window, *la finestra*,
that all your vocabulary flies,
  the agitated nouns, the melodious adjectives,
the verbs like squat men with thick legs
  trudging down dusty roads after market day,
the sky dark, the first stars glimmering
  uno, due, tre, so few you know
that you will never be able to count them.

Al Fresco, Caro

The thing I love most about being in Italy
        are the picnics,
a stroll to the *mercato*, the *forno*, the *enoteca*,
        for *carne*, a loaf of bread, *vino rosso*.
Did I say cheese? A soft one, Bel Paese,
        or hard, *pecorino*, and *prosciutto*,
        olives wrapped in waxed paper,
        fruit—*fichi, pesche, melone*.
We hike to the Piazza San Marco, take the number seven bus
        to Fiesole and trudge up the hill,
nearly killed by two Fiats, a Renault,
        and a swarm of Vespas.
It's hot, we're tired, but we find a dusty patch
        and spread our blanket.
The thing I love most about being in Italy
        are the naps,
under the strolling clouds but inside, too,
        two beds pushed together,
their legs tied with twine.
        What would life be without siestas,
long afternoons of sleep, beckoning from
        the fury of work,
or on a hillside, weary under the fierce
        September sun?
We eat, we talk, we eat, a grape in one mouth,
        a slice of *mortadella* in another,
        then wine or water or wine.
The thing I love most about being with you
        is that my body, so often an encumbrance,
becomes the vehicle of such pleasure
        that the whole cannot be contemplated,

so I close my eyes and imagine your arms,
        from the beginning the object
        of my sincere admiration,
the portion above the elbow, beneath the shoulder,
        freckled, shaped like an eggplant,
sweet as a peach, a pear, not edible exactly,
        but something that the teeth can define,
and the lips, poor parched thin flaps of skin
        to be turned to such divine employment.
Oh, that every job were so rigorous,
        so fraught with intellectual joy.
But you are the busy one—industrious, even.
        What are you doing?
        "I'm doing," you say, "something."
We are lying on a blanket, a spread,
        on a Tuscan hill, the light marching
over cedars and pines like soldiers off
        to some inconclusive skirmish with the horizon.
Are we hungry? I am under the impression
        that we have eaten.
"I need nourishment," you cry, taking a *melone*.
        We are hungry.
The thing I love most about being in Italy,
        besides eating out of doors,
is eating out of doors, parched mouth
        to parched mouth, scorched arms, searching blind
for that other one who eats, talks,
        thinks, breathes the same air,
though alone, really, and deliberate as light.

St. Barbara of the Dog Bite

Santa Barbara, sublime and generous protector,
I implore you to separate from me those wicked
and miserable beings who wish to interrupt
my Christian life.

         —prayer from a votive candle

If I were to list my enemies, dogs would not top the list,
     nor would people, though they irritate me upon occasion;
no, thoughts, my own primarily, are my foes,
     erupting from nowhere
     like new volcanos from the ocean floor
or more often like suppurating boils but with voices
     because my opposition is in constant communication with me,
blabbering on about my vagaries, various villainies,
     peccadillos, misdeeds and depravities.
Do you believe that every action has meaning,
     that even the activity of a gnat has a symbolic resonation
     throughout the universe,
that every inhalation has two incarnations:
     one its bump and grind through the material world,
and the other a silent sonic boom
     through the collective unconscious?
Well, I do, too. The problem is interpretation.
     What does it mean?
Anyone with the I.Q. of a hedgehog knows that though a rat's
     sneeze is fraught with significance for the rat,
it is probably not all that relevant for godlike you and me,
     so when I am vacationing in the north of Italy
     with my beloved,
staying in Alba with friends of friends, a lovely couple,
     cultivated and bookish who have a little dog,
a dachshund to be precise, whose name is sZnoopy,
     or that's how the Italian "S's" come out,

and the four of us are lingering over our post-prandial grappa
       after feasting on truffles and lamb and cheese and Barolo,
and I reach down to pet the seemingly benign sZnoopy, who
       until that moment has been groveling in the manner of dogs,
and in a flash of pure evil, he snarls,
       draws back his malevolent lips, and fastens his teeth
       upon my left breast, what does it mean?
At the moment, I am too horrified to think. I stand up,
       scream, clutch my bosom;
gravity detaches sZnoopy, but on the way down or up
       (depending on your point of view)
he nips my right thigh, left knee, right calf,
       drawing blood on the thigh.
It is a tableau of horror, like a Caravaggio composition,
       backlit and overblown.
I am screaming, sZnoopy is yipping, our host and hostess
       are clucking.
Mortified, they exile sZnoopy to the gulag of the kitchen;
       they pat me, they comfort me,
but it's only the beginning: a few days later in Antibes
       a monstrous German shepherd lunges at me,
his insane owner cackling while unenergetically pulling back
       on the leash,
and the next day in Aix-en-Provence, Twisty the apricot toy
       poodle of the hotel concierge
fastens her tiny satanic teeth to my ankle. I shake her off,
       and she skids across the polished floor of the lobby
and thumps her little cranium on the wall.
       "*Pauvre Twisty, le pauvre petit,*" everyone whimpers
       while I drag my leg behind me to the elevator.
Then in Arles a mutt tries to jump from a moving car
       to savage me,
and in Avignon a Rottweiler takes an enormous shit
       on the sidewalk and I step in it,
       ruining my beautiful metallic gold Italian sandals.
Have you noticed? All dogs, all in cities beginning
       with the letter "A."

I admit I'm superstitious, but I think this bears closer
        scrutiny. Why dogs? Why "A"s? Why me?
I remember St. Rocco, who always appears with a dog
        and is pointing to a huge gash on his thigh.
Okay, so he wasn't martyred by a dog's bite, but it's possible.
        I think of my own martyrdom with dogs
        and the resulting work of art:
I'd be looking up at heaven and pointing to the bite mark
        on my breast, around my feet sZnoopy, Herr Shepherd, Twisty,
the mutt from Arles, and the Avignon Avenger, all snarling
        or shitting.
Oh, the artist would have to have a fine hand
        to do justice to my wounds:
the five bruises of St. Barbara, the growling, defecating curs
        circling my hem.
I see an angelic light streaming from a break in the clouds,
        putti puffing around my crown, my gown morning-glory blue.
I am looking for my Caravaggio, always.

St. Anthony of the Floating Larynx

We take a train to Padua to see the Giottos, lapis and gold,
and the mostly-destroyed Mantegna frescoes of the life

of St. James, blown to bits by a wayward American bomb, patched
together like a puzzle now, but with most of the pieces missing.

My friend is on a pilgrimage to the Cathedral of St. Anthony
of Padua, patron saint of harvest, lovers, sick animals,

and lost objects, *oggetti* in Italian, and this church
is quite an *Oggetto* itself, with a capital "O,"

and I have seen my share of shrines in the last three months.
Immediately I recognize that this is no ordinary repository

of frescoes, plastic statuary, and other divine bric-a-brac.
It is a hive of religiosity, alive with bizarre reliquaries;

in fact we stand in line to see St. Anthony's larynx, yes indeed,
his voice box, suspended in a gelatinous scarlet liquid,

a cartilaginous snake of animal matter, from which my husband
(educated by Jesuits) turns, white as a piece of typing paper.

This is the Italy I dreamed of, saints, snakes, gypsies,
cutthroats in a baroque tutu of religion and sin.

The venality of it all is like eating cake for breakfast,
though it's obvious that not much cake eating is going on

in the Cathedral of St. Anthony but rather atonement for cake eating,
for three quarters of the multitude in the church

are on their knees, reminding me of a Billy Graham Crusade
I attended as a twelve-year-old when the great man himself said,

"Fall down on your knees and pray for God's forgiveness."
It's an interesting concept, forgiveness, and one, I must say,

that appeals to the throng in Padua, or are they praying
for miracles? In a sense forgiveness is a miracle, or at least

for someone like me who finds pardon difficult and unfulfilling,
or as my friend Mary Ann Wolf used to say, "What good's a grudge

if you can't hold it?" What would St. Anthony have to say about mercy?
I wonder as I queue up with my friend at the saint's tomb.

She wants a husband and I want back the bag that Alitalia lost
three months ago in Rome. As I raise my arm to place my palm on

the wall of the tomb, a four-by-four grandmother dressed in black
cuts in front of me and knocks my arm out of the way.

Her problem is probably a lot more pressing than a suitcase
of dresses, which, by the way, St. Anthony delivers to me

a month later in the Miami airport. My friend is still single,
although her old boyfriend called and told her she was

the love of his life, not exactly her dream come true
but in the true-love ballpark. Maybe the saints do better

with material requests. A green silk dress has got to be easier
to deliver than a boyfriend with a job and a working personality.

Metaphysics is so tiring, which is what St. Anthony would
probably say if he could, lying in that tomb, sans larynx, teeth,

and assorted other body parts. Day after day, we line up with
our problems, raise our troubled palms. "Maria? No, my friend, she's

wrong for you. It won't last more than a year." And the poor guy
goes off, thinking, That Maria, I could really be happy with her.

The Beatification of St. Lucy

St. Lucy is probably everyone's favorite saint, not simply
because she's mine but because her virtues are unassailable,

primarily that she most often is depicted holding a plate
on which rest two eyeballs, hers, as a matter of fact, although

she always has two in her head as well, and this is not even her miracle,
although what great event led to her canonization

this researcher was unable to ascertain. Being raised Protestant,
I suspect the pope or a gaggle of medieval cardinals, sinister,

with shifty eyes, of hiding the truth about the beatific Lucinda
from the rabble, the outcasts, the scrabbling incontinent hordes,

that is to say, you and me. A voice from my metaphysically
fundamental *maison natale* screams, "There was no miracle."

Ah, but I know differently, for there is always a miracle if you know
where to look. Or what is art, which is Lucy's message, if you think

about it, those weird unconnected eyes rolling around on saucers.
How I love her name, in all its forms: Louisa, Lulu, Lucia, Lucy.

How lucidly it slips from the tongue, plummeting like a waterfall
of syllabic perfection. What, then, to return to the subject of our

inquiry, was the curious occurrence, the miraculous circumstance,
astonishing, extraordinary, unaccountable, divine event

that led to the beatification of this simple if ocularly gifted girl?
 Coming from a theological background that does not

accentuate hagiography, I find myself unprepared for the leap
of imagination, the occult surge necessary to solve this enigma.

Loaves and fishes? Already done and with panache. Ditto, water
into wine. So what is our adorable girl left with? The obvious—

restoring sight or something terrible or *terrible*, as the French
would say, two words which, although spelled the same, I use in

the French sense as something filled with terror and beauty,
an utter rearrangement of natural laws, as in a cataclysmic rending

of the organic veil, that is, levitation or mechanically unassisted
aviation, or more interestingly, a collusion with time as in the case

of the Hysteron-Proteron Club, a group at Oxford in the twenties
whose members, inverting the sequence of a day, would wake in

white tie and tails, light Havanas, and drink whiskey until it was time
to dine, beginning with dessert. Yes, it is my contention that

for a few moments in the fourth century, the creaking caster of time
was reversed, and morning crept back into the cocoon of night,

dreams rolled from their dreadful conclusions to their innocent,
bucolic openings, and the night unlocked its splendor.

Radiant night, velvet convoluted conjunction of dark and light
in which Lucy reigned peerless in the starry sky until

the priests grabbed her around the throat and her eyes popped out,
not a poetic conclusion but one that is gratifyingly anti-clerical

and would include all dissenters and Round Heads as well,
but the Reformation was more than a thousand years in the offing,

merely a bad taste in the mouth of God, conceived by that arch-misogynist
Martin Luther who would poison passion for generations

of *innamorati*, condemning us to formica kitchens and birch-lined dens, in
which we remember vaguely, over casseroles and Monday Night Football,

that distant Eden when our eyes were swimming with apocalypse,
revelation, our other eyes staring at God knows what.

St. Clare's Underwear

You can see why men are such monsters
      when you look at a woman's body,
Devonshire creamy from a bath,
      or just the general curviness
      of the whole design.
Then there's your average man,
      hirsute and raging with testosterone,
Godzilla *incarnato*, King Kong with big feet,
      Frankenstein hovering
over some delectable damsel with skin
      like fresh pastry.
So you can see why St. Clare threw in her lot
      with St. Francis, a nice guy,
      good with animals,
although there were rumors. But aren't there
      always?
In Italian, the word for noise is *rumore*,
      which is what gossip is,
though why women should be thought
      more inclined to tittle-tattle than men
      is a mystery to me,
but not something I was thinking about
      one evening in Florence
      as my husband and I strolled
      along the Lungarno Soderini
and in the Piazza Cestello happened upon
      a theatre presenting Goldoni's
      The Gossip of Women,
though after one act I felt that it could have
      as easily been called *The Foppery of Men*.
My dear, the prancing and smirking
      that transpired,
      and in a country known for its machismo.

When the young lover puckered his carmine lips,
            the men in the audience were making a noise
that sounded for all the world like laughter,
            though one can never be certain.
I learned something that night,
            though exactly what, I'm not sure,
and my education continued in Assisi
            where we saw glass cases with the clothes
            of St. Francis and St. Clare,
            sandals and sackcloth,
though Clare's case contained what looked like
            a rough slip or chemise.
"St. Clare's underwear," I cried with such happiness
            to my husband,
            but by that point he was sick of me
and my non-Catholic lack of respect for everything
            he no longer holds dear.
In Italy you are either *cattolico* or *acattolico*,
            which, I imagine, makes Anglicans
            and Four-Square Gospel Pentecostals
            rather uneasy bed partners,
as, I suppose, hermaphrodites and transsexuals
            are made anxious by the words
            "woman" and "man."
I like to think of Kierkegaard's idea
            of the natural home of despair
            being in the "heart of happiness,"
which could mean any number of things,
            such as black is not black or even white,
or that we are all as confused as Dracula,
            dreaming of a local milkmaid, her C-cup,
            coarse lingerie, ruddy cheeks,
and the blood, of course, always the blood.

Borromini's Facade

Across the Piazza Navona from where I sit
      stands Borromini's concave and austere facade
      for the church St. Agnes in Agone,
but I am so stupid that I think it is St. Agnes in Agony,
      as in Bernini's hypererotic St. Teresa in Ecstasy,
      which I saw the afternoon before,
an angel staring at swooning Teresa's heart,
      yet aiming his spear a little bit lower
      than the seat of all emotions.
In Rome the 17th century was a time of intemperance,
      of popes in ermine re-imagining the city
      through baroque eyes—
      Carracci, Maderno, Caravaggio, Bernini—
so one can imagine a dejected Borromini standing
      in the Piazza Navona,
elliptical living room of Rome, built in 86 A.D.,
      often flooded for mock sea battles
and still used in the 17th century though by that time
      for less bloodthirsty entertainments.
One can see Borromini here, his meticulous heart
      filled with what?
      Revenge? Shame? Divine inspiration?
Behind him looms the Fountain of the Four Rivers
      by his arch rival Bernini,
the commission stolen from him with the connivance
      of Olympia Maidalchini, "sister-in-law"
      to Pope Innocent X,
the fountain a brilliant concoction of stone
      and water and light,
piercing Borromini's back like the angel's arrows leveled
      at St. Teresa's mons veneris
while he surveys the pathetic church
      that had been begun by Carlo and Girolamo Rainaldi,

originally the site of a brothel and the miracle of St. Agnes,
  whose name means lamb in Latin,
and who at thirteen was sought by the young swains of Rome
  for her beauty and wealth.
Ah, but Agnes had other ideas,
  as is so often the case with young girls,
and replied to these bumptious suitors
  that she had pledged her virginity to a heavenly husband
who could not be seen and conveniently enough
  did not possess fleshy lips wet with saliva
  as did her suitors
when they denounced her as a Christian
  to the Emperor Diocletian,
not a notable fan of that sect but who,
  because she was a rich girl,
  asked her to rethink her position.
One look at the knot of her accusers
  must have been enough to keep Agnes faithful
  to her incorporeal lover,
for she was soon sent to the bordello in the arena,
  the very spot upon which I am gazing,
with an invitation to the riff-raff of Rome
  to abuse her as they would,
but when Agnes was forced to strip for said pack of curs,
  her hair grew to cover her nakedness.
Poor chicken, she was beheaded, miracle or no,
  the Romans bored by wonders.
And Borromini nearly 1400 years later
  covering the mediocre Rainaldi church
  with a facade so exquisite
that it is an architectural equivalent
  to the spiritual purity of St. Agnes,
whose agony was much like that of her architect,
  over-scrupulous in an age of excess.
Borromini killed himself by falling on a sword,
  molto giapponese,
while Bernini lived another twenty years,

and given the choice,
I must admit that Bernini's way is more pleasant,
    though I don't like to think of myself
    as one of the sybaritic churchmen in theater boxes
that he placed on either side of the niche
    containing the delirious St. Teresa.
I imagine their lips quite as wet as those
    of St. Agnes's paramours, a pack of older dogs,
    to be sure, but dogs nonetheless.
It's the old mind-body problem again,
    or the mind-dog problem,
    which Agnes and Teresa approached,
each in her own peculiar fashion:
    Agnes saying no to the dogs,
    Teresa saying yes to God,
and Borromini screaming while he writhes
    on the floor of his *appartamento,*
    a bloody mess, his servant shrieking,
the neighbors running to gawk and gossip,
    as the artist clutches his wound,
the room dimming, the curve of the day
    like the arc of his building,
sublime, mathematical, pulseless, cool, and dark.

Wild Greens

Green, the sky above Florence, sodden
with threat of flood, and a young woman sells

little bundles of wild *rughetta, rucola*
in the damp tangle of the Sant' Ambrogio market,

while across the Ponte Vecchio in Santa Felicità
is suspended Pontormo's *deposizione*, the shadows

on St. John's torso lime, acid green as the faces
of the vegetarian girls, Tina and Jackie,

standing horrified under umbrellas at the tripe
vendor's wagon on the Via dei Cimatori,

pale green, as the pistachio *gelato* at Vivoli,
after midnight, dark green, as the steep incline

of the Oltrarno from the windows of the Uffizi,
green as the soggy leaves on the pavement

of the Piazza Santo Spirito after the market
and two weeks of a rancorous *sciopero*

by garbage collectors, blue green, the scarf
of the beautiful violinist in the Teatro Verdi,

a wisp of aquamarine in the sea of black and white,
green, the swaying trees outside a restaurant

in Maiano, their loose leaves stuttering
like the arms of excited children running

in the drizzle of dusk, and the Arno, raging, water
tarnished bronze, verdigris, its banks lined with visions

of inundation, as green as the eyes of the woman
selling wild greens in the market, her brown skin,

her smile an orchard with regular fruit,
rows of apples, ripe pears, Bosc and d'Anjou,

queues of bitter herbs, dense, tart,
raw as the damp morning, biting my face and hers.

Nose

I am trying on an especially evil-looking pair of shoes
when the shopgirl points to the middle of her face and says,

"This is called what?" For a moment I draw a blank as I search
my mind for the Italian word for snoot, schnozzola, beak,

but when "il naso" finally surfaces, I realize
that she is Italian and probably knows the Italian word

for nose, so what she wants is the English,
which is relatively easy for me, so I say, "Nose."

"Nose," she replies, smiling. "You have a beautiful nose."
I am looking at the shoes on my feet. I have dangerous feet,

especially in these particular shoes, but my nose
is rather white bread, too much like my skinflint grandmother's

for me to ever be entirely ecstatic about it,
and this girl's is spectacular, an aquiline viaduct

spanning the interval from her eyes to her delicious lips.
A friend once told me, "My sister paid $2,000

for a nose like yours, a perfect shiksa nose,
but it ending up looking like Bob Hope's."

Suddenly, I feel as if I have no nose, like Gogol's Kovelev
riding around St.Petersburg looking for his proboscis.

What is a nose? Obviously not simply a smeller, sniffer,
or a mere searcher out of olfactory sensation,

but something more—an aesthetic appendage to the facial
construction, a slope from brow to philtrum,

with symmetrical phalanges. Aren't I precise, who knows precisely
nothing about having an unsatisfactory nose, or ever thinking

about it for one second? Perhaps my offending part
is somewhere else, or am I as hapless as Gogol's hero—

with too little nose for my purposes, like Miss Ruby Diamond,
the richest woman in my town, who lost her nose to cancer,

and had two counterfeits, one lifelike and the other
a simple plastic flap to hide the scar of ninety years.

A nose is a nose is a nose is a nose,
Gertrude Stein did not say and why would she

as it is obviously untrue? Though each nose is an island
in the sea of the face, sticking out in a more or less

inadequate fashion. Like Cyrano, I marshall my couplets,
ragtag though they be, to celebrate all noses unloved,

those lost to disease or, like Kovelev's, inadvertently
misplaced, and the nose of the shopgirl on the Via Roma

in Firenze, her eyes red from either smoking pot or heartbreak
and the many other indignities gathered like humps on our backs,

which we touch for luck, as if floods, bombings, murders
could only happen to others who are beautiful and pure.

Skin

In the Museo di Storia della Scienza in Florence
        is a room whose walls are lined with dozens
        of wax models of women's uteruses,
illustrating just how many things
        can go wrong in childbirth.
Those babies don't have a clue about how to be born
        and are coming out arms akimbo,
        feet first, bottoms up.
I have never seen anything as scary
        as the model with a lone foot
        sticking out the vaginal opening.
The men in the room, I notice, are discussing
        everything quite scientifically,
but the women are a different story,
        as would be the story of science, I imagine,
if women had not been taken up with having creatures
        ripped out of their bodies
        every sixteen months to two years
until they either died or by the miracle of plague
        or old age their husbands did.
The vaginal opening is really quite small
        and an infant's head enormous.
The mathematics of this seem incontrovertible,
        or is it geometry?
Numbers are no help, and there seems to be no science
        to describe this *tristezza*,
not sadness exactly but something so close
        that it would be the word
you'd choose to describe the longing
        to be lost in the body of another—
        the smell, the touch, the skin.

Delirium

Just before I fainted in the restaurant that evening,
 I was telling you a story about a madman
 I saw earlier in the day
as I walked home from my ballet class
 just off the Piazza Santa Maria del Carmine.
After crossing the bridge of Santa Trìnita,
 looking in at Ghirlandaio's frescoes
 for the Sassetti family,
then wondering how many women there were
 who were young and rich enough
to wear the see-through lace cowboy shirts
 in the Gianni Versace windows
 on the Via Tornabuoni,
at the intersection of the Via de Calzaioli
 and the Via del Corso,
I walked into a hullabaloo being drummed up
 by a bearded man who was stalking back and forth,
 screaming something in Italian, of course,
 and waving his arms in the air.
But when he turned he would reach down with one hand,
 clamp his crotch,
 and then pull his body around
as though his hips were a bad dog
 and his genitals a leash he was yanking.
After each turn he'd continue stalking and flailing,
 until time to turn again.
So I am trying to explain this and our pizza comes,
 and I saw off a bite, but it is too hot,
so what do I do but swallow it, and it's too hot,
 and I think, it's too hot,
and my voice decelerates as if it is a recording
 on a slowly melting tape and the scene
 in the restaurant begins to recede:

in the far distance I see the bearded man ranting
        on the street,
then nearer but retreating quickly you
        and the long corridor of the restaurant,
then it's as if I am falling into a cavity behind me,
        one that is always there, though I've learned to ignore it,
but I'm falling now, first through a riot of red rooms,
        then gold, green, blue and darker
        until I finally drift into the black room
        where my mind can rest.
I wake up in the kitchen, lying on a wooden bench,
        with you and the waiter staring at me.
"I'm fine," I say, though it's as if I am pulling
        my mind up from a deep well.
The waiter brings me a bowl of soup,
        which I don't want, but it doesn't matter because
the lights go out and a man at the next table says,
        "*Prima quella signora ed ora la luce,*"
which means, first that woman and now the light,
        and it's so dark that I can't see myself or you,
and I feel as if I'm turning, a mad voice
        rising from my stomach
crying where are we anyway, and who, and what, and why?

Dust

Remember Hamlet's speech to Rosencrantz and
        Guildenstern,
"What a piece of work is a man?"
        You know the one,
where he's dicking around with them
        and at the same time taking a dive off
        the deep end of his own melancholia?
Don't we all feel like that sometimes,
        smart and suicidal at once?
It's like drinking Mai Tais and doing differential
        calculus at the same time;
you're fine until the rum hits your cerebral cortex
        like a blunt instrument,
then you're Professor Plum in the Library
        with a knot the size of a naval orange
        on the back of your head.
Old Hamlet asks, "What is this quintessence of
        dust?"
Dust—it's a dry word, with Saharas of space
        between each letter.
I thought about dust a lot when I was a girl,
        its etiology and how to stop its blitzkrieg
        through my room.
To dust or not to dust. "You must dust," said
        my mother, but why?
Why not stop it before it starts, in fact,
        suppress dust, abort it?
But I soon realized stopping dust was synonymous
        with stopping everything.
That's what it always comes down to: death.
Death to all tyrants, including time, tide,
        and entropy, as in the exquisite second law
        of thermodynamics.

You learn about it in school and then go right
        ahead and plan your snug little future.
The glorious entropic future. I suppose I'm
        shedding my skin at a normal rate,
        contributing to the general flakiness
        of the planet.
But dust. Anything worthless. What about gold
        dust? Think of Chaplin eating his shoe.
Dust. Have you finished dusting? Yes. Dust.
        A dreamy word, fairy dust, moon dust,
        deliver me from all that is ashes to ashes,
Dust to Derrida and all makers of books both great
        and small, dustcatchers in dustjackets.
Oh, you can do your best to remain unencumbered but
        what's the point because
Encumbrance is the name of the game,
        or en-cucumbrance,
because sex is one of the major building blocks
        of those prison walls.
Sex and folly. Are they the same? Sometimes, yes,
        and sometimes, yes.
Once I went to Paris without my husband,
        and I wrote him that I missed his courgette.
How did I know that arcane piece of French slang,
        he asked?
I felt so smart, so French, so dustless.
What isn't folly? And what doesn't lead
        to disintegration of some kind?
"I fall to pieces," sang Patsy Cline, which is what
        Hamlet was saying in a more roundabout
        Elizabethan way.
There's that—the flaking skin, the breaking hearts,
        plane crashes, sword fights,
        fights over money, autos-de-fé,
        an armageddon here, an internecine skirmish there.
Dust makers, one and all, biting the dust,
        licking it, making it fly,

shaking it into the night sky
which looms mysterious with its dusting of stars,
        and grants a kind of clemency
        to the whole set-to,
as would anything so immense and utterly remote.

Deception

I am at a party in which the usual suspects
        are gathered around their usual subjects
with their familiar gin and tonics, chardonnays,
        cheap beaujolais, and for the former drinkers
        and present vegetarians, club sodas.
I am standing near a nice couple, really approaching
        them to chat when I see a woman pass,
        a woman I know well.
She smiles at the man. That smile and the look on his face
        tell me immediately that some hanky-panky has transpired.
A man does not look at a woman that way unless
        he has had sex with her.
It's an expression with an equal mixture of lust
        and sickness unto death.
This is a pattern I have seen over the years: her husband,
        a married boyfriend. Different husbands, different
        boyfriends.
Freud would call this a repetition compulsion.
Would this man care if he knew? Probably not.

Knowledge is funny and has very little to do
        with anything, except after the fact
        and maybe not even then.
Do you think that Anna Karenina would have gone back
        to her husband if she had had the chance?
Even as much as she loved her little Sergey?
        I'd say no, but then I'm not Tolstoy.
I think of our first hideous years of marriage,
        the nadir of which was your three-year-old son
        screaming, "You're not my mother."
I remember thinking, "No kidding,
        and what makes you think I want to be?"

It was horrible, and I was happy. Which makes it a little
        easier to explain this party
and my quickly mounting despair.

Half an hour later, I see the woman in the kitchen
        with her arm around her husband.
Poor schmuck, she gives him the same smile that she gave
        her boyfriend, but at a considerably lower voltage.
Well, I suppose someone has to be the husband.
The boyfriend's a husband, too, but I don't think
        the husband is a boyfriend.
I think he's a drunk blowhard
        who can be nice on occasion.
Oh, what do I know? Maybe he's the love of someone's life,
        maybe even his wife's,
        but I don't think so.

The love of my life—
how would this translate into Bantu, for example:
        the one who brought seven cows
        and forty goats to my house?
Or Hindu: god who fathers a thousand sons?
Or Inuit: citadel of blubber, quick as a silver fish?
How would you describe me? I take my glass of red wine
        and run off to find you,
but you are talking to the former best friend
        of your ex-wife,
and I see an enemy, twice-removed, who I dodge
        out of habit.
Drink up, me hearties.

Later, on the patio, I see the same smile pass
        between the woman and her former boyfriend,
        who is a major blowhard but goodlooking
        and smart if you like the know-it-all type.

Oh, I am in a bad mood. It's the cheap wine and the underwire
of my only black bra, which is digging into the soft skin
of my right breast.
What I wouldn't do for glass of Pouligny-Montrachet
and a kiss from your sweet lips,
a kiss like the first one,
softer than any breast or breath, when we were deceiving
everyone—ourselves, perhaps, most of all.

Doubt

"Don't use that teleological argument on me,"
      you say to your mother.
You are fifteen, only beginning your long slippery
      descent into skepticism.
It's ugly at first, like a new baby, red, sticky,
      screaming, keeping you up at night,
but soon it begins to plump up, coo, grow eyelashes
and what was once heresy turns into nihilism,
      which is French, looks good in black,
      has thin lips with a *bon mot* on each one.
Doubt is anxious, bites at her lip, but wears
      beautiful shoes, pointed and to the point.
You read Sartre, drink absinthe, listen to Billie
      Holiday sing "I Cried for You," stay up all night,
      sleep till noon.
You have a job but you leave one day and never go back.
      You're not sick exactly but rather sick of it.
Money is a problem, but money is nothing and nothing
      is everything so you are rich, a plutocrat
      of minutes and hours and days.
You read Russian novels into the night,
      and you become confused. Are you Kitty Shcherbatskaya
      or Natasha Rostova or Prince Myshkin?
Outside the window, is it your street or the steppes?
      It's cold, and doubt keeps you warm
      by its cozy little fire.
But something goes wrong. You fall in love with a boy
      who believes everything.
This is rich. You scoff at his dogma,
      but how can you love him?
What is this fly-by-night disturbance in your chest?
The sex is terrible, because he says you believe

in nothing, but you know nothing makes sex better
than nothing, letting your body fly
        into the dark midden of disbelief.
You hear music in the street, in the uneven surface
        of the afternoon.
Too hot the sun falls like a plague of light, squandering
        its heat on a world of uncomprehending surfaces.
What is it that you love? You cry, "I don't know.
        I don't know."
And it's funny but you don't, and you tell him that doubt
        is oriental, Chinese to be precise,
and he can kind of get it, but in the end you're bored,
        and he is *de trop*.
"What do you want?" he cries. It's what they all finally ask
        when you can't stand them anymore.
"Not your skinny inauthentic ass, that's for sure,"
        you think. Or say, depending on how fed up you are.
But you reflect upon it sometimes, what you want, I mean.
        It's not life after death or an ersatz immortality
in the form of a little bundle of joy,
        and you have the perfect black dress.
No, it's something in you, what you want to be or do or say,
        not courage or anything like that,
but to be thrown into prison and know the lyrics
        to all the Motown hits from 1962 to 1973,
        including "My Guy" and "Ain't Too Proud to Beg."
It would be important for morale, maybe even start
        an insurrection
because you suspect that more than anything,
        life is like a play by Samuel Beckett,
        which is to say it's sometimes funny and always weird,
and when the lights go out and the curtain closes,
        you want be someone who could stand alone in the dark,
look into the face of God and say,
        "You look like him, but let's see the wounds."

III

The Autopsy of John Keats

—for Phyllis Moore

To Italy

On September 17, 1820, Joseph Severn, an artist, left London, accompanying the dying Keats to Rome.

London had already turned gray when we set sail,
    the *chiaroscuro* of architecture,
        the drab shadow of stone,
etched line of branches in the cinderous sky,
    color leeched of its brilliance—
        yellow into ochre, brown to dun,
green to moss, crimson to rust—
    the slate sky choked with ash-colored clouds,
        rumbling, threatening, breaking,
washing pigment from cornice and pediment.

My liver was giving me trouble;
    I pictured it a rebarbative rodent,
        foxy, sable-tipped, brown ears like brushes,
dripping umber, burnt sienna. Where is the liver?
    Above the stomach or below?
        I lay in bed, visualizing
the inside of my body a dark rust color—
    mahogany blood, toast-colored organs,
        darkened as if in a forest fire,
spleen the shape of a filbert, heart the color of a walnut.
    I would step out of my skin and spread it on the sheets
        like coffee-colored velvet, a spongy canvas,
examine the inner lining of my life, never seeing myself
    standing there, a skeleton, topaz bones
        strung like a Christmas tree with snapping rats,
nuts, bloody strands of gristle and flesh.

The hellish sea showed no mercy,
  at first smooth as an eggshell,
   a lake of blue glass, no wind,
only lavender clouds punctuating the amethyst teacup
  of the sky, and when we're finally off,
the water rising like an empty mouth,
  blue madder and ravenous,
   the sky falling down to meet the furious waves
until everything is liquid, dark,
  stars falling to rest on the ocean floor like anemones,
   our ship climbing the walls of water,
skating down the other side to the sad sweep
  of the Mediterranean, the coast of Africa a wafer
   in the dull blue distance.

Just after sunrise, we sailed into the Bay of Naples,
  the crimson sky inflamed with a passionate sun.
   The seven sins clambered into boats
and rowed out to us, women with faces like cherries,
  men with scarlet caps and scarves,
   selling fruit, bread, meat, *dolci*;
Vesuvius with its creamy clouds florid in the morning light,
  the sea claret, boats filled with flowers—
   roses, carnations, poppies.
We searched out the shore for Herculaneum,
  Pompeii, Sorrento, the horizon paling
   into a soft and iridescent rose.

Four black months in Rome—*novembre, dicembre, gennaio,*
  febbraio—our rooms dark,
   my heart like a piece of coal,
smoldering, the days short, the last month
  four ravens perched on the window sill,
   their yellow beaks a question
but I had no voice, my hand trembled as I tried
  to write an answer in someone else's hand
   in ink as black as night.

Death is pale when you see it, like milk in a glass bowl,
    the pallor of nothing, cold to the touch,
        like snow on the chalk cliffs of home.
A face bleached of all meaning, silver, marmoreal,
    lying without breath frosting the nostrils,
        nothing, *niente*, no color,
just the alabaster chill of lifelessness,
    as if the receding blood were moving away
        from this poor vehicle into the vast ivory sea
from which it came, from another world, a pearl we've forgotten.

Roma, gilded metropolis of God, the duomo of St. Peter's
    like an egg yolk reflected
        in the blond water of the Tevere.
Months pass and the light changes,
    the jaundiced sun of winter turns amber,
        peaches ripen, faces become less sallow, smile,
turn to me in the honeyed air with flecks of gold
    pouring from the sky, saffron detritus of the gods,
        straw-colored morning, tawny night,
in my hand a blood orange from Sicily, so sweet
    it could make me forget, restore me,
        open my eyes so I might again see.

Mrs. Pidgeon Writes to Her Daughter

My dearest Eleanor, We arrived at Gravesend at noon
      and there our progress ended. Captain Walsh
wished to set sail that night, but the weather
      was unfavorable, so we were forced to stay
the next day. I must say my accommodations
      leave much to be desired. I do not blame him,
I assure you, but your dear husband William
      will want to know (in the event he is asked
by another person or relative to reserve a space
      on a sea-going vessel) that a darker, smaller,
more disagreeable cabin has, I am sure, never been
      inhabited by six persons. My fellow travelers
on this voyage are. . . . Well, let us say they
      would not be my choice of companions. The cabin
allows for six, three tiers with two beds apiece,
      one atop the other, although Captain Walsh
and the mate are never in the room during daylight
      hours for which I can only be grateful,
as they are ghastly men, rough and sullen.
      You will be appalled to learn that two
of the persons I share these dismal quarters
      with are dying of consumption. A young man
and a young lady. You know, my dear, the aversion
      I have for the sickroom. It is quite all
I can do to maintain my dignity and composure
      in the midst of the physical disintegration
that surrounds me. Of the two young men,
      one is a poet and the other an artist. The poet
is the dying man, and a rude, wag-tongued fellow.
      The other, a Mr. Severn, is little better.
They talk and laugh about nothing as far
      as I am able to discern. Miss Cotterell,

the young lady, faints hourly. Mr. Severn
          seems to expect me to come to her assistance.
Can you imagine? On Tuesday the sea was very rough.
          I have never been more miserable in my life.
We were in our beds all day, green, unable to eat.
          Captain Walsh informs us that we will sail along
the coast line to skirt the rough seas.
          The two young men have gone ashore several times
with Young Miss. I must say, she and the dying man
          are high-spirited. I would not have made this voyage
for the world, except that I could not allow
          my darling Isabella to go through her first lying-in
at the mercy of papists. I am sure I do not know
          if there is an English physician in all of Italy.
Isabella is so brave, insisting that she would be
          perfectly well without me. Without her mother
at a time such as this! I suspect that Mortimer
          was behind these words for between you and me,
Eleanor, I have never thought that he was quite our kind,
          but of course Isabella must please herself.
I'm sure I was too easy with her, with you both,
          but that is my way. I have a soft heart.
I will post this from Portsmouth where we have docked
          for a few hours. Give my love to William
and to the children, I remain your affectionate mother,

                              Ellen Pidgeon.

Captain Walsh Contemplates a Storm
in the Bay of Biscay
While Keats and Severn Cower Below

A violent conflagration of water and wind
      brings out the philosophy in a fellow,
   for, though sailors are an irreligious lot,
  impending death sands the calluses off a heart
     faster than any evangelical frothing and fasting.
It's fear, I fear, that fastens us to God;
     who knows if he intends it? I suspect
   we are like barnacles on his hull,
  so when the sky turns a nasty purple
     and an unpleasant silence dissolves over the scene
no malice is intended, instead I prefer to see it
     as a disinterested fury or a turbulent disorder
   in the weather, much like a headache in a
  particularly muscular farm animal whose horns,
     though cruel, are not intended as such
but are nonetheless capable of grievous injury
     to the body and by extension the soul, for
   what is the soul without the flesh but ether
  or some such other useless thing? If, indeed,
     God is responsible for the weather, then I'll
not be putting my faith in him, I'd rather put it
     in a well-built vessel, a collision of metaphors,
   for God is the ship if you recall my previously-
  expounded theory, much in the same fashion
     that the whale was Job's ship, which implies
God ate Job. If not, He ordered it, and
     a captain must take responsibility for his ship
   or whale or whatever the hell he's sailing
  the high seas to perdition in when the water boils
     over, capsizing the senses, irradiating
the sky in a riot of thunder and terror and light.

Lt. Sullivan Amuses Keats during the Quarantine
in the Bay of Naples
(with Interjections by Death)

Captain Walsh
(in the ship's log):   After four weeks and three days, we have
reached Naples. An uneventful voyage,
although we nearly lost the ship during a
storm in the Bay of Biscay, what!

Severn (on deck):   Napoli. From the sea it is a paradise. White houses
swarm the hillsides, nestled in vineyards and olive
groves, and to the south Vesuvius sending out
clouds of smoke that metamorphose into chimeras,
then drift toward Sorrento. The sea has shaken off
the sickly green of the Atlantic and been transformed into an indescribable blue, a lapis, azure, a
deep sapphire. . . .

Mrs. Pidgeon: I loathe Naples. Too many colors, like a harlot or a
harlequin. Not a moral city, I'll be bound. No
wonder Mortimer chose it for my darling Isabella.
What are those boats coming toward us? I hope
they are not filled with dirty Italians.

Lt. Sullivan: The Union Jack, do you see, boys? Let's row
over and pay them a visit.

Miss Cotterell: I am so weak. My arm feels as if it were carved
in marble. I cannot lift it. My head is heavy as a
pumpkin squash, my poor brain is beset by fever.
Where is my brother? Do I see a boat with baskets
of fruit? Bring me a peach for my parched throat.

The Fruit Vendors: Arance, ciliege, fichi, fragole, limoni.

Bureaucrats of Napoli:	Signori, signore. Scusi. In London, c'è typhus. You must stay on the boat for dieci giorni.
Severn:	Ten days!
Bureaucrats of Napoli:	Si, signori. Dieci giorni. Arrivederci.
Death:	Typhus in London! Delizioso. How a plague lifts the spirits. I hope they're dropping like flies—delightful insects, so industrious. Ah, nothing like a sea voyage. Two are mine—the girl and the scribbler. Perhaps I'll take the old baggage's new grandchild or better yet the daughter. Serve her right for having such a tedious bore for a mother. Her kind lives forever.
Lt. Sullivan:	Hallo! Hallo! I'm coming on board.
Captain Walsh:	Sir, we are under quarantine.
Lt. Sullivan:	Oops, too late.
Bureaucrats of Napoli:	Dieci giorni.
Miss Cotterell:	Look, in that boat. It is my brother. Shout to him (my voice is too fragile). Warn him of the quarantine.
Lt. Sullivan:	(Very loudly.) Beware, sir. We are sequestered on board for ten days. Typhus in London, what.
Mr. Cotterell:	Oh, dear.
The Fruit Vendors:	Mele, cocomeri, lamponi, pesche, prugne, uva.

The Neapolitans in boats:	Dov'è il signor inglese che è pazzo?
Bureaucrats of Napoli:	Eccolo.
Mr. Cotterell:	I believe they are referring to you, Lieutenant.
Lt. Sullivan:	Si, sono pazzo. To be rid of my duties for ten days in such jolly company.
Mrs. Pidgeon:	Will I never be rid of these baboons?
Death:	Unfortunately for said simians, no. Only the years and the ingestion of too much mutton will make you ripe for my scythe.
Miss Cotterell:	Oh. The air is too fragrant. It is too heavy for my poor weak lungs.
Death:	I hate the complainers. She is going to hang on for two years, sighing and fretting. If one were executed for being boring, Miss Cotterell would fall even before the fat one, because nothing is less charming than enervation. There she goes again.
Captain Walsh:	Catch Miss Cotterell.
Lt. Sullivan:	I have her.
Mr. Cotterell:	(From his boat.) Oh, dear.
The Fruit Vendors:	Fichi, albicocche, arance, fichi, fichi, fichi.
Lt. Sullivan:	Mr. Keats, do you know the Italian word for fig is also the word for the secret parts of a woman?
Severn:	Fichi.

Keats:	Fanny.
Lt. Sullivan:	No, the other side.
Keats:	I fear, sir, you are a baboon.
Lt. Sullivan:	(Holding up an orange.) Or an arancia-tan. Such delectable globes of ambrosia! Have you ever seen such fruit in London?
Keats:	Oh, for an English spring, an English apple.
Mrs. Pidgeon:	Here, here, sir.
Keats:	On second thought, I believe I will join you. Che cosa è questa? (Holding a bunch of grapes.)
Lt. Sullivan:	(Fanning Miss Cotterell's insensate face.) Uva.
Keats:	Uva. Ova.
Lt. Sullivan:	Who's the baboon now?
Keats:	I feel Dionysian.
Lt. Sullivan:	Ah, vino. Il vino rosso, signore. That will put you right.
Keats:	To your good health.
Lt. Sullivan:	To yours.
Death:	Ha.

Keats' Disease Addresses Him in the Voice of Mr. Lovelace, Nemesis of Clarissa Harlowe in the Eponymous Novel Which Keats Finishes Reading (in Nine Volumes) the Night Before He Leaves Naples

Villa di Londra, November 6, 1820

I have been thinking of late on the occasion
of our meeting. You believe our first encounter
was through your brother Tom. Not so,
though it suited my purposes for you to think it.
You are fatigued, delirious at times,
your memory is not strong. Think back to Scotland,
to the tour you took with Brown, walking
between Inverary and Oban, the rain falling
like a cold blanket—we were trudging
to the same inn, a mean place that served up eggs
and oakcakes, which you could not bear.
We drank together, *whuskey*, as the Scots say,
and a bonny drink it was, the spirit mixed
with water and sugar, though it could not calm
your throat, raw as the wind over Loch Awe.
Do you remember now? The room was dark.
Ten men crowded the hut. I don't suppose you do.
You met me again as Tom's constant companion. A sweet boy.
Molto sensitivo. You see I have been studying the language.
And now you lie in this meager bed, bewitchingly noble.
You hate me, loathe me, fight against me at every turn.
I am patient. You will call out to me one day,
begging me to come, pleading with me to take you,
beseeching me like a lover. You are half in love with me now.
Throw this volume down as you did Byron's *Don Juan*.
Your temper is diverting. I admire your courage.
Most lie supine and flutter their hands like distracted
insects in the summer heat. Naples is a filthy city.

If you don't leave soon you will surely expire.
Roma è la più bella città teeming with contagion
and antiquity. You are surprised that aesthetics
interest me? I am a polymath, a scientist of sorts,
a mathematician, one might say, though the odds
are decidedly in my favor. You think me brutal,
unmerciful. It's true, mercy has little place
in my game; however, I can be subtle, astute.
In your case, I have arranged everything
to your advantage, given you your fondest wish,
if you must know, for in not so many years
you will be greater than certainly your contemporaries.
Of course, no one can eclipse Shakespeare,
but you will be mentioned in the same breath.
You are so ungrateful. What is it about the human
condition that makes its dissolution so painful?
It seems a muddy, ignominious, uneven venture to me.
Some have more to lose than others, I grant you.
Yet if I were to play the clairvoyant for a moment
and tell you that you have written your greatest poems,
would not you fall into my arms gladly? No?
I will never comprehend this. You have no choice.
I believe my scenario is exceptional. You will, in time,
acknowledge it to be so. Sleep now. It's late
and the journey to Rome will be difficult.
When you arrive it will be my pleasure to show you
the various sights. One walk I know you will enjoy.
The views are breathtaking: ah, me, the antiquities,
le vie nobili. Until then, *arrivederci, carissimo.*
You must trust that I am your most sincere
and devoted admirer, &c.

Keats and Severn See Something Unusual

Seven days from Napoli
  we enter the Campagna of Rome,
a vast sea of towering saffron grass.
  In the distance a dab of crimson,
a speck of red on an ochre canvas.
  Nearer, the fleck achieves outline,
becomes a cardinal,
  potentate of the Church,
shooting small birds,
  the irony lost on the afternoon,
vast and impassive blue
  over billows of undulating grass.
Sparrows. Christ spoke of them,
  but absented now from divine protection
or subject to the higher need
  of ecclesiastical sport,
they fall from the sky.
  An owl flies tied to a stick,
mirror attached to his collar
  corralling his kind in, to their
end. Two servants gathering birds,
  loading guns. Hundreds falling,
uccelli morti, morti, morti,
  among the autumn blossoms,
wild in the tall grasses,
  that spread on until Rome appears,
the Eternal City,
  world without end, amen.

Dr. Clark Examines Keats upon His Arrival in Rome

The body is a box of marvels, a prodigy, a rarity,
      for no matter how often I look into it,
prod it, poke it, pretend it is dross,
      a mere confluence of cellular movement,
the body answers with its own astonishing perfection,
      not to mention symmetry,
that lovely connivance between left and right.

Like a bottle, the body holds mysteries we can only guess at,
      a nebuchadnezzar of vinegar or elixir,
a jeroboam of fluid,
      for the body is foremost liquid, water in fact,
though at times champagne may gain ascendancy
      in the veins of the frivolous.

I think sometimes of the body as a plate on which all things
      scrumptious and grotesque are served—
boil or beauty mark, éclair or tapeworm—
      yet the human form is not without contour,
its very convexity, its curves, arcs, whorls, parabolas
      being the base of its most ancient and firmly held wish
for divinity, Corpus Christi, corpus delicti.

The body is a traveling bag, a valise of organs
      and cerebral matter, a trunk of blood,
a rucksack of indigestion and dyspepsia,
      a portfolio of consumption,
a reticule of cancerous longing.

When we are children it is a table, for we dress it with linen
      and smear its surface with jam.
But as we age, the body becomes a repository,

          a safe full of ragged debris,
the flotsam of this and that, who and when, front and rear.

The body contains something I cannot describe beyond flesh,
          has a modus operandi that is elusive though explainable;
it admits, takes in, accommodates, expels, sweats, demands,
          refuses, drinks, contemplates, breathes,
          and it is this breath, fragrant and infectious,
that troubles me, it is like inviting your most virulent enemy
          to sleep with you, in your own bed, your soft bed
in the center of your house, but only after making sure
          his blade is sharp and he never sleeps.

Signora Angeletti Discusses Her Two Boarders (with recipe)

Olio is the key, from Lucca, near Firenze;
      I never use anything else, and for this dish,
my specialty, *spaghettini con pomodoro e basilico*,
      I use *una mezza tazza*, and I believe this is the secret
of its sublimity, because though a simple recipe
      and nourishing, it achieves something of the infinite,
if one can say such a thing about food.
      I must explain that I judge a man by two things:
the way he eats and the size of his feet.
      A woman cannot be happy with a man who has big feet.
I cannot tell you why, but I know it is so.
      Large feet are an abomination before God,
for there is nothing more ridiculous
      than a man walking down our noble avenues
with feet the size of fishing boats.
      And by the same logic, a man who does not eat
is not a man. Take the sniveling English artist.
      You'd think he was a chicken, peck, peck, peck.
Now I tear the *basilico, una tazza*, each leaf
      into three or four pieces, and chop very fine
the garlic, *due cucchiaiate*, and put both in a bowl
      with the *olio* and add to this the crimson *pomodori*,
peeled and diced. The artist (his feet were enormous)
      did not like my pasta, would sneak around, move
furniture at three in the morning, meow like a cat
      when we passed in the street. What kind of man
is this? The other was dying. I could see it
      immediately. Of course, he had no interest in food,
but to his credit his feet were *piccoli*, dainty
      almost like those of a *marchesa*. Another secret
is in cooking the pasta, just a minute, no longer, one second

too long and the dish is ruined, a little salt,
due etti di prosciutto, tossed in with the *pomodori*
and *basilico*, and of course *vino rosso*,
which our Lord, as his first miracle, made from plain water,
an injunction, I have always believed,
to all good Christians to drink deeply on any occasion
as we are carried through this world
on our nefarious appendages, both large and small.

Lt. Isaac Marmaduke Elton and Keats on La Principessa Borghese (née Pauline Bonaparte), Marble and Flesh

What do two rather priggish Englishmen circa 1821
think, that is what opinion do they have,

of the libidinous, show-off sister of Napoleon Bonaparte,
a woman who is married (most agree in name only)

to Prince Camillo Borghese and who does precisely
as she likes, unlike the blushing bourgeois belles

upon whom the poet and soldier have fastened their
affections? Oh, not much, but then again quite a bit,

for not only do they pass her on their daily walk
along the Pincio, they have seen Canova's marmalade

sculpture and pronounced it exquisite if ever so vulgar,
which, of course, it is. One suspects immediately

upon seeing it that Pauline believed her breasts
to be *trop belle* and being a generous sort of girl

wanted to share them with everyone and especially
the devilishly handsome Lt. Elton. Both young men,

consumptive *in extremis*, have been advised
not to excite themselves, that is, take carriage rides

to the Colosseum and the Tivoli Gardens, which on any
scale cannot approach La Principessa, with her eyes

like nougats, arms like loaves of fresh bread,
she is an arrow of erotomania, so you can imagine

how anxious these two young men become,
how apprehensive, for if piles of rubble could cause

a debilitating fit of coughing, surely an intimate
encounter with the delectable Principessa Borghese

could easily rob them of life itself, so after she
makes it clear that Lt. Elton is her intended victim,

they decide to abandon the Pincio for another less
paulinish walk, limbs aquiver, voice boxes quavery,

two high-minded young men, who, one suspects,
had less fun than la bella Paulina, though one

wrote better poetry, and the handsome other,
who, by the skin of his teeth, escaped her snares

to live two years longer in a neutral country
with tall mountains and doorsteps that were

each morning fastidiously scrubbed by women
with large arms and cheeks like wholesome fruit.

Severn Falls Asleep

Death crawls closer
        on nights like these,
    the chill creeps in
and hangs on the walls
    like curtains.
The fire dies,
    the candle is eaten
        by its weak fluttering flame.
    My eyes close.
I have sat up so many nights
        with him
    they fall together
        into one long stream
    of darkness that flows
through my veins,
    rattles in my ears
as his breath rattles
        in his chest,
like a child's toy
    but darker
        and more slowly.

The Autopsy of John Keats

On Sunday the second day Dr.
Clark and Dr. Luby with an
Italian surgeon opened the body.

—*Joseph Severn to John Taylor*

One heart, small ferruginous organ the size of a dinner roll;
　　　domicile: the bosom, the breast, hub of the human organism,
　　　　　central terminus for the arterial system, the blood,
cells both red and white with their particular functions,
　　　chest open like an untidy nest in which lies
the object so insignificant, seat of unspecified longing,
　　　to ache, to break, to beat, to burn at last with bitterness.

Two lungs, like remnants of pink silk, tattered bloody cloth,
　　　hem of a ruined ball gown, shredded taffeta,
torn magenta satin, after dancing, laughing—running
　　　　　through stormy avenues, to damp fields, lying down,
returning to a world unchanged but so altered
　　　as to be unrecognizable, shoes ruined, delirious,
　　　　　unable to breathe, impossible,
lungs gone and all the places, adored and loathed, gone,
　　　　　the last inhalation caught in the trees
　　　of the Villa Borghese, or tangled in the chandelier,
forever in that room, small, unwarmed by sunlight,
　　　once two lobes the size of bread loaves,
　　　　　one larger than the other.

One liver, darling companion of champagne and claret,
　　　toasts drunk to your health, no to yours,
at Haydon's immortal dinner, Charles Lamb drunk as a lord,
　　　　　voting his host not there and forcing Wordsworth

and the others to drink his health;
in Scotland with Brown, the whiskey drunk near the grave of Burns,
    the harsh *vino rosso*, brown with bile.

One spleen, to digest insults, hatred, jealousy, penury;
    Z railing in *Blackwood's*—Return to dispensing pills
and salves; Brown's valentine to Fanny Brawne,
        not that but her delight in it;
Abbey's niggardly grip on the purse strings,
        letting Tom die, forcing George to emigrate,
and money in the end so essential, so vital,
        weak pound of the blood, pound sterling, pound of flesh.

One stomach, memorial to meals resplendent and meager,
      roast ducks, boiled vegetables, mutton, beef, beets,
        bread—coarse and fine; the sauces of memory,
Christmas sauces, sweet, savory, the goose with its fatty sheen,
      pudding with a blue brandy flame,
so the final hunger when it comes is raw and mercenary,
      presses like a leech, a bloodsucking, carnivorous mouth,
        bleeds the body of all it once was.

Two hands, in the autopsy room digging like a miner,
      turning pages of Milton, Shakespeare, trimming a quill,
 wiping Tom's brow, at last in the hands of Gherardi,
        mask maker for Canova,
oiled flesh, transparent, cold under plaster.

Two feet, grey birds, delicately boned wings furled
    close to their backs as in sleep or arched for flight.

Two eyes, large, *i due occhi*, liquid, tranquil,
    like the darling children of an indulgent mother,
        perfect, curious, forward.

Two ears, wild hedge roses, single helix of silken pink,
    anti-helix, concha, incus, Eustachian tube, the inner ear,
        avenue to the dark dream of the brain,
unruly throng of memory: the quiet of Enfield,
    the pandemonium of London, Brown's booming basso profundo,
        Haydon's light tenor, Abbey's scrabbling stingy whine,
    Mrs. Pidgeon's caterwaul, Dr. Clark's rational drone,
Severn playing Haydn on the rented piano,
        Fanny Fanny Fanny Fanny,
her voice faint as a child's vacant memory of a song,
    melodic, sweet, selfish,
rocking in a little boat, sailing into sleep.

One mouth to speak in a language perhaps unknown,
        to study forgotten verbs,
conjugate tenses that tell us what we might have done
        at some fixed time in the past,
to describe what we believe we have seen,
        what we think may be true.

One mouth, two lips, two leaves to the house of longing,
    well of pleasure, vortex, black chasm of the universe,
the volcano of intellect erupting with words no woman can hear,
        no man can understand,
to kiss, to press one's lips against another's skin,
    to feel with one's lips the texture, rough or soft,
        of another being.
Her skin, scent like a ripe peach in June,
        taste—the flavorless ambrosia of everything
one cannot have, to touch her lips, to drown
    in that mortal sea again, lost, salt on the lips, parched.

One heart, small rust-colored organ, *il cuore,*
       the piazza of the body, a spacious open place,
under the moving baby blue Tiepolo ceiling,
    the duomo of heaven, where one can walk for a little time,
talk with friends, survey the passing scene, sit,
      drink from a cup a liquid that is bitter but delicious,
a short, hot drink that enrages the blood
    for a few hours and then passes into nothing.

One mouth, two lips closed, as if abandoned.

One body, lying without memory, a pale thing, a specter,
    a congregation of cells,
the pale silk of skin a miraculous cloak
      for the impedimenta of being.

Two eyes, two ears, two hands, one stomach, one mouth, two lips.